# Nicholas Heller

# THE TOOTH TREE

 Greenwillow Books, New York

**TO ALEXANDRA**

Watercolor paints and a
black pen line were used
for the full-color art.
The text type is ITC Bookman.

Printed in Singapore
by Tien Wah Press
First Edition
10 9 8 7 6 5 4 3 2 1

Library of Congress
Cataloging-in-Publication Data
Heller, Nicholas.
The tooth tree / by Nicholas Heller.
        p.      cm.
Summary: In the backyard
where Charlie has buried
his tooth because he no
longer believes in the
Tooth Fairy, a voracious
tree covered with teeth
grows up and begins to
devour everything in
sight, but all is saved
by the bedside appearance
of the Tooth Fairy.
ISBN 0-688-09392-2.
ISBN 0-688-09393-0 (lib. bdg.)
[1. Tooth Fairy—Fiction.]
I. Title.
PZ7.H37426To      1991
[E]—dc20
90-39791      CIP      AC

"Look," said Charlie after dinner.
"My tooth has come out!"

"Why, so it has," said his father.
"Don't forget to put it under your pillow
for the tooth fairy," added his mother.

"Oh, I don't believe in the tooth fairy anymore,"
said Charlie. "That's for little kids."
"Shhh!" warned his father. "Don't let the fairy
hear you say that. You'll hurt her feelings."

Charlie went outside to play in the yard.
"There's no tooth fairy," he said to himself.

But just in case, Charlie dug up his secret treasure chest, where he kept his three best marbles, his troll, and his device for communicating with aliens, and he put his tooth in as well.

There, thought Charlie, as he flattened out the dirt.
Now it will be safe. And he went in to bed.

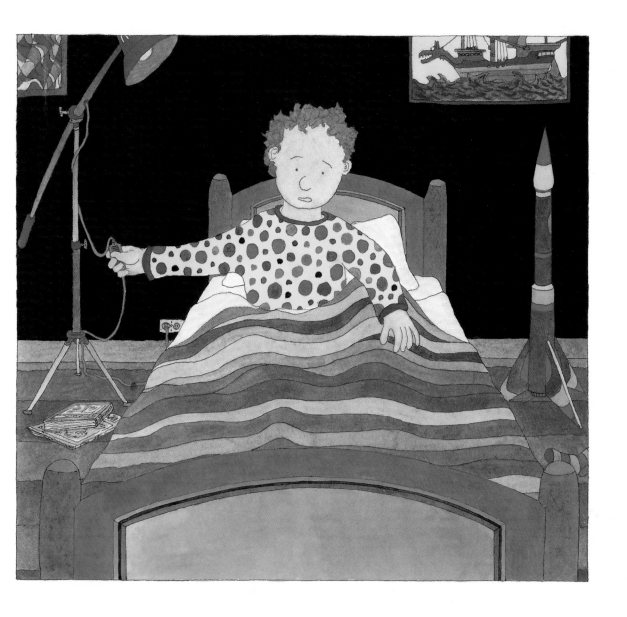

Some time later, in the middle of the night, there was
a funny noise. What could that be? Charlie wondered.

Charlie looked out his window and saw, right where
his secret chest was buried, a very odd-looking plant.

It was making squeaking noises and growing bigger and bigger, right before his eyes!

Instead of leaves on the ends of its branches,
it had teeth, and it was starting to eat things.
First it ate the sprinkler,

and then it ate some shrubbery.

Then one branch ate the birdbath and the
badminton set, while another one reached over the
fence into the street and started eating a mailbox!

"Uh-oh!" said Charlie, as a branch slipped past his shoulder into the bedroom and began munching on his rocking chair. "I'd better go wake up my parents."

"No, wait," whispered a voice. "Don't do that."
Charlie looked around in surprise, but he
didn't see anyone.
"I mean, there's no reason to alarm them,"
the voice continued. "I'll take care of this."

"Who are you?" asked Charlie. "And where are you?"
All he could see was the branch, which had finished
his rocking chair and was about to swallow his
geography book.

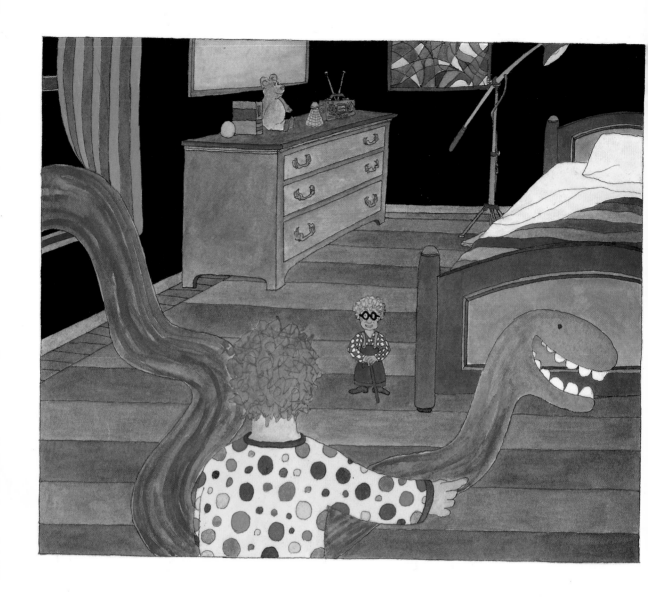

"I'm the tooth fairy, and I'm right in front of you!"
Charlie looked down, and there she was.
"Hello, and what's that thing?" he asked, pointing
to the branch, which was headed happily in the
direction of his closet.

"It's a tooth tree, naturally," answered the fairy. "What do you expect if you go burying your teeth in the backyard instead of putting them under your pillow where they belong?"

"I'm sorry," said Charlie. "And I'm sorry I said I didn't
 believe in you."
"That's all right," said the tooth fairy. "Some people
 really don't. Now get back into bed. I will take care of
 the tree."

Charlie got into bed, and the tooth fairy jumped up
on his dresser.
"Tooth tree, tooth tree, return to the earth!" she cried,
waving her arms through the air. Then she said
some magic words that Charlie couldn't understand
but that made him feel, all of a sudden, very sleepy.

In the morning, Charlie ran down to the yard.
The sprinkler was back, and so were the birdbath
and the badminton set.

But when Charlie dug up his secret treasure chest,

he discovered that his tooth was gone,
and in its place was a shiny quarter!